FOR PIET

and all the children in Iowa.

Library of Congress Cataloging in Publication Data
Quackenbush, Robert M.
   Sherlock Chick's first case.
   Summary: Hatched from his egg with detective's hat
and magnifying glass, Sherlock Chick immediately sets
out to find who has stolen the corn from the chickens'
feed bin.
   [1. Mystery and detective stories. 2. Chickens—
Fiction] I. Title.
PZ7.Q16Sk 1986 [E] 86-9398
ISBN: 0-8193-1148-0

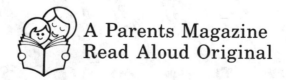 A Parents Magazine
Read Aloud Original

SHERLOCK CHICK'S
FIRST CASE

by Robert Quackenbush

PARENTS MAGAZINE PRESS · NEW YORK

The minute their chick was born,
Emma Hen and Harvey Rooster
knew that he was special.
He popped out of his shell
wearing a detective's hat.
"We'll call him Sherlock,"
said the proud parents.

Sherlock Chick's first words were,
"Are you in need of a detective?"
"Yes, we are," said Emma Hen.
"You've come just in time!"
She pointed to an empty
feed bin in the chicken yard.
"Someone has taken our corn!"

Sherlock Chick went
with his parents
to the feed bin.
"Who do you think took
the corn?" he asked.
"We don't know," said
his parents.

"I will look for clues,"
said Sherlock Chick.
He walked around the feed bin.
"Aha!" he said.

What did he see?

He saw a trail of corn.
It was leading out of the yard.
"I will follow this trail,"
said Sherlock Chick.
"I will find your corn
and bring it back."

"That's our boy!"
said his parents.

Sherlock Chick followed
the trail of corn.
Suddenly, he stopped.

What did he see?

He saw a horse.
"Do you like corn?"
asked Sherlock Chick politely.
"No," said the horse.
"Grass is my favorite
thing to eat."

The horse had not
taken the corn.
So Sherlock Chick
went on his way,
following the trail.
He stopped again.

What did he see?

He saw a goat.
"Do you like corn?"
asked Sherlock Chick politely.
"It's all right," said the goat.
"But eating the paper off cans
is much more fun."

The goat had not
taken the corn.
So Sherlock Chick
went on his way,
following the trail.
He stopped again.

What did he see?

He saw a pig.
"Do you always eat your
corn on the cob?"
asked Sherlock Chick politely.
"Yes," said the pig.
"The cobs are my favorite part."

The pig had not
taken the corn.
So Sherlock Chick
went on his way,
following the trail.
He stopped again.

What did he see?

He saw a scarecrow.
"Do you like corn?"
asked Sherlock Chick politely.
"I never touch it,"
answered the scarecrow.
"I'm here to chase crows away.
They like corn a lot."

"Aha!" said Sherlock Chick.
"I think I know who took
the corn from the
chicken yard."
He hurried on his way.
The trail of corn led to
an old barn and stopped there.
Sherlock Chick peeked
through a crack in
the barn door.

What did he see?

He saw three crows.
They were pecking away
at a pile of corn.
It was the corn from
the chicken yard!

Sherlock Chick had a plan.
He ran and got the horse,
the goat, the pig, and the
scarecrow to help.
They went with him
to the barn.

The horse put the scarecrow
next to the barn.
The goat knocked down
the barn door.
The pig ran through the barn
squealing, "Oink! Oink!"
as loud as he could.

The crows flew out of the barn
and right into the scarecrow.
"Awk! Awk! Awk!" they cried.
They were so scared that they
flew away and never came back.

Sherlock Chick and his friends
brought the corn back
to the chicken yard.
"This case is closed,"
said Sherlock.
Emma Hen and Harvey Rooster
were so happy to have
the corn back
that they had a big party
and invited everyone.

And that is the end of
Sherlock Chick's first case.

About the Author

When Robert Quackenbush's son, Piet, was very small, he was curious about everything. In fact, he liked to walk around with a magnifying glass so he wouldn't miss anything! Remembering this helped Mr. Quackenbush create Sherlock Chick.

Robert Quackenbush has written and illustrated over 40 picture books for children, including the popular Henry-the-Duck series for Parents. He has received many honors for his work, including a nomination for the Edgar Allen Poe Award for best children's mystery. In addition to creating picture books, Mr. Quackenbush owns an art gallery in New York City where he teaches painting, writing, and illustrating.

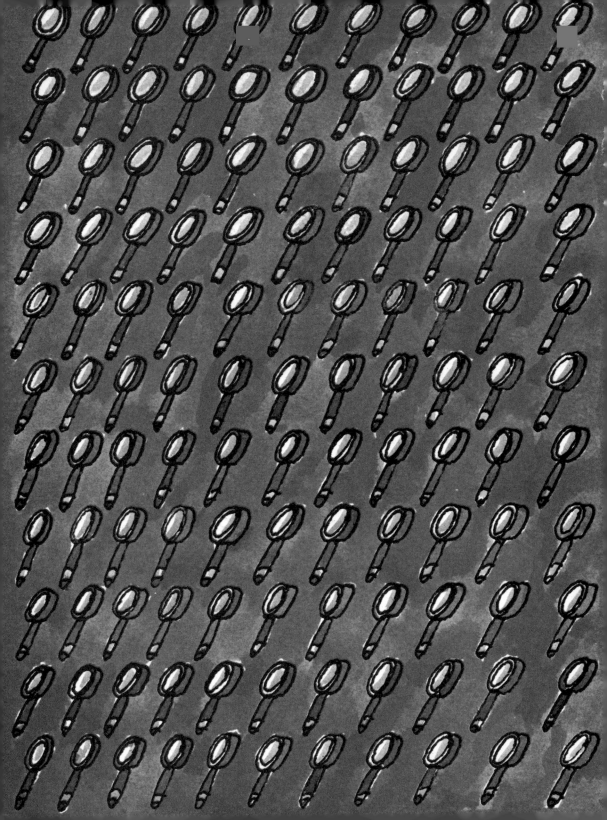